BIG BAD BUBBLE

WORDS BY

Adam Rubin

PICTURES BY

Daniel Salmieri

ANDERSEN PRESS

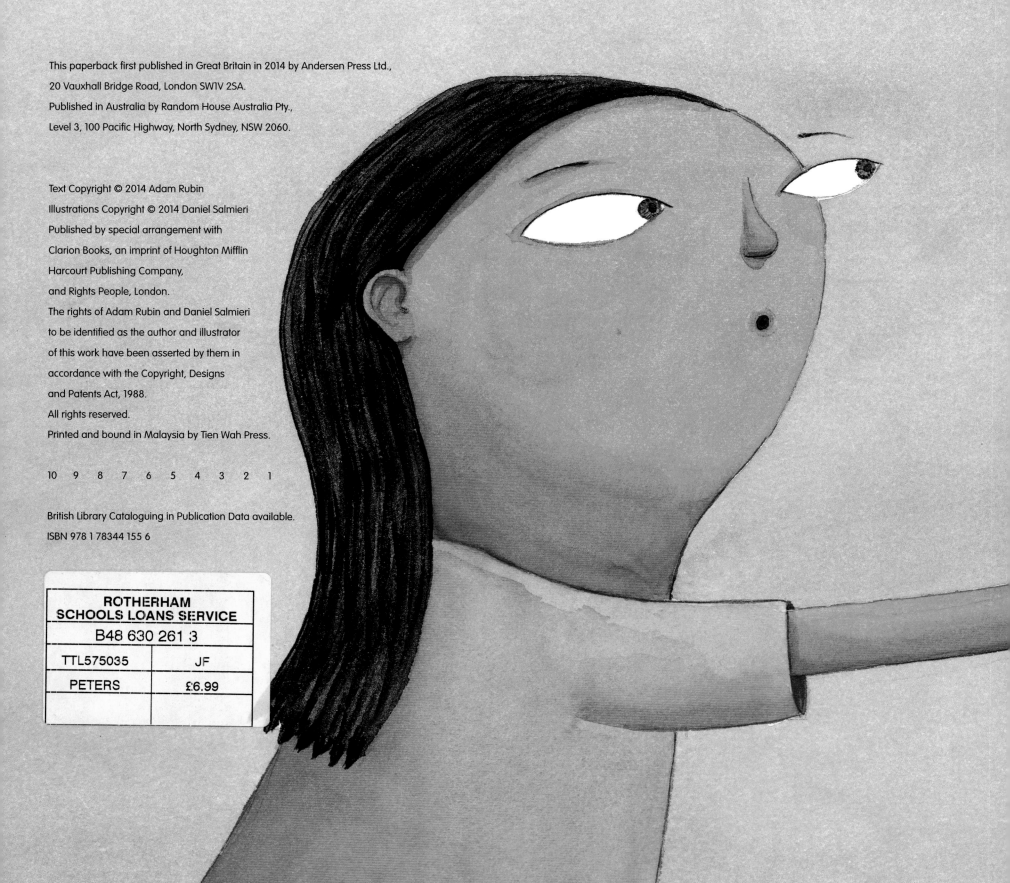

This paperback first published in Great Britain in 2014 by Andersen Press Ltd.,
20 Vauxhall Bridge Road, London SW1V 2SA.
Published in Australia by Random House Australia Pty.,
Level 3, 100 Pacific Highway, North Sydney, NSW 2060.

Text Copyright © 2014 Adam Rubin
Illustrations Copyright © 2014 Daniel Salmieri
Published by special arrangement with
Clarion Books, an imprint of Houghton Mifflin
Harcourt Publishing Company,
and Rights People, London.
The rights of Adam Rubin and Daniel Salmieri
to be identified as the author and illustrator
of this work have been asserted by them in
accordance with the Copyright, Designs
and Patents Act, 1988.
All rights reserved.
Printed and bound in Malaysia by Tien Wah Press.

10   9   8   7   6   5   4   3   2   1

British Library Cataloguing in Publication Data available.
ISBN 978 1 78344 155 6

ROTHERHAM SCHOOLS LOANS SERVICE	
B48 630 261 3	
TTL575035	JF
PETERS	£6.99

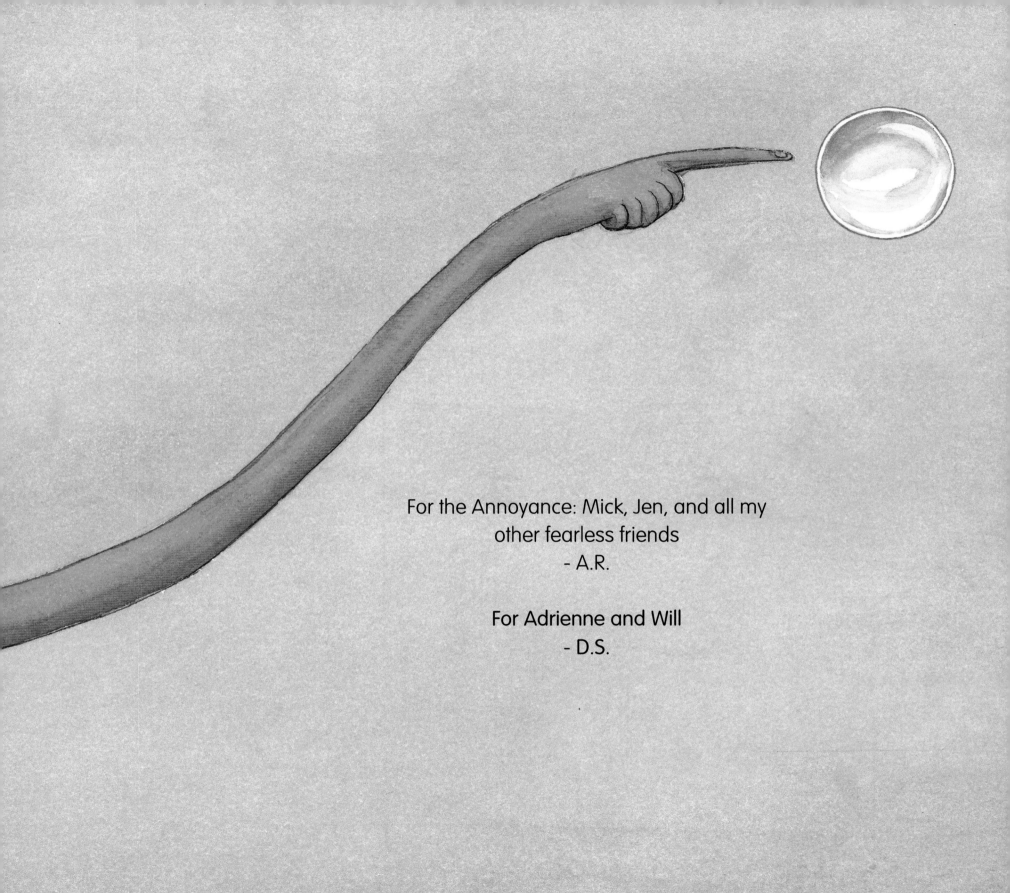

For the Annoyance: Mick, Jen, and all my
other fearless friends
- A.R.

For Adrienne and Will
- D.S.

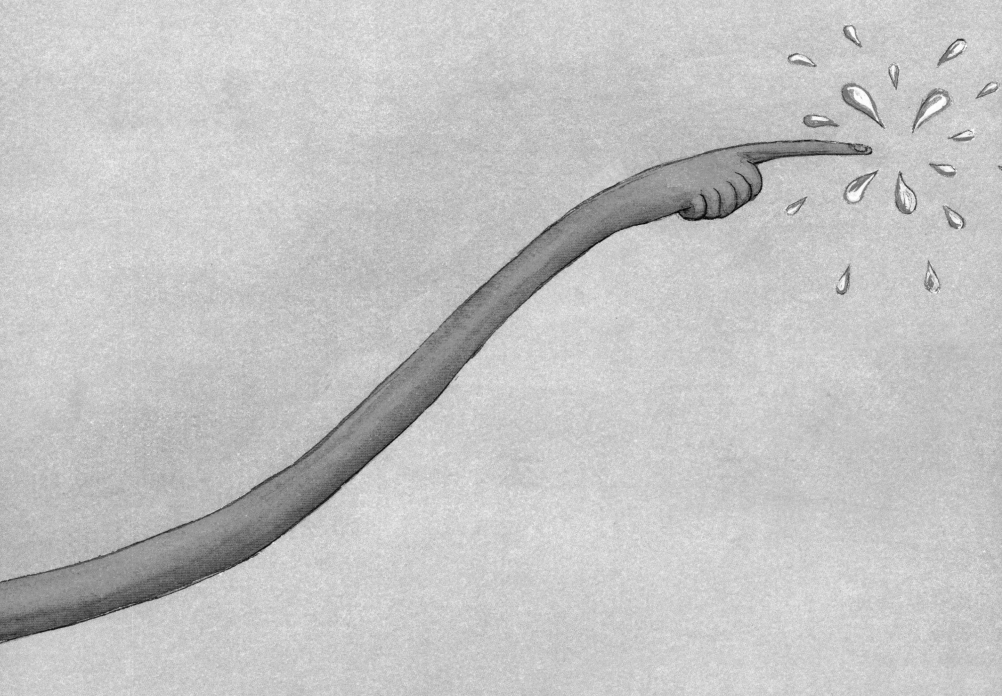

YOU may not know this, but when a bubble pops, it doesn't just disappear.

It reappears in La La Land . . .
where the monsters live.

For some reason, all the big, scary monsters are terrified of bubbles.

Froofle, why are you running away?

Yerburt, what's the matter?

Turns out, it's all Mogo's fault. When he was little, a chewing-gum bubble attacked his face. Since then, all he can talk about is how dangerous bubbles are.

Bubbles are sneaky. You never hear them coming.

Where there's one bubble, there are many bubbles. They travel in packs.

Summer is the worst time for bubbles. That's when they go into a feeding frenzy.

Don't listen to Mogo. He has no idea what he's talking about.

I'll admit it's a bit surprising when a bubble suddenly appears out of nowhere. But that's part of the deal with living in La La Land. On the plus side, doughnuts grow on trees, and the rent is cheap.

FOR RENT
£26 per month

Hey, look! Here comes a bubble now.
Yerburt, stop running around in circles.
You have giant fangs.

Froofle, climb down from that tree.
Look at your claws. You have pointy claws.

Wumpus, get out from under those covers.
You're much too big for that bed anyhow.

Look, here's a bubble. It's just a thin layer of soap and water wrapped around a ball of air. It's soft and delicate. It couldn't hurt a fly.

You could pop it with a little finger.

See?

Froofle, use your claws.

Wumpus, don't be scared. It's just a teeny, tiny . . .
oh, wait. That's kind of a big one.

See? Mogo doesn't know what he's talking about. There's no reason to be afraid.

Enjoy your bubble gum, Yerburt.

Have fun popping your bubble wrap, Froofle.

Oh, boy, that is a big bath full of bubbles, Wumpus!
(Tell Wumpus to save some water for the fish.)

Fine, maybe bubbles aren't so dangerous after all. Butterflies, on the other hand...